Raven's Orcha

RAVEN IN THE CITY

Patricia Harris

illustrated by
Lorna Williams

HABA®

PowerKiDS
press.

NEW YORK

Published in 2018 by The Rosen Publishing Group, Inc.
29 East 21st Street, New York, NY 10010

First Edition

Managing Editor: Nathalie Beullens-Maoui
Editor: Theresa Morlock
Book Design: Michael Flynn
Illustrator: Lorna Williams

Cataloging-in-Publication Data

Names: Harris, Patricia.
Title: Raven in the city / Patricia Harris.
Description: New York : PowerKids Press, 2017. | Series: Raven's orchard | Includes index.
Identifiers: ISBN 9781508161479 (pbk.) | ISBN 9781508161493 (library bound) | ISBN 9781508161486 (6 pack)
Subjects: LCSH: Ravens–Juvenile fiction. | City and town life–Juvenile fiction.
Classification: LCC PZ7.1.H36 Rav 2017 | DDC [F]–dc23

Manufactured in China

CPSIA Compliance Information: Batch #BS17PK: For Further Information contact Rosen Publishing, New York, New York at 1-800-237-9932

Please visit: www.rosenpublishing.com and www.habausa.com

CONTENTS

Raven loved his home in the orchard, but he was curious. He decided to visit the city.

It took him most of the day to get there.
He was hungry when he arrived.
He looked and looked for some fruit trees.

Raven flew into a park. He found some delicious sunflower seeds. He ate enough so he was not hungry anymore. He left many seeds on the ground.

The next morning Raven went back to the park but he did not find any more seeds. While he was looking around for seeds, six chipmunks ran by going in all directions.

Raven decided to try to find a new garden. He flew away from the noisy roads. He saw many big buildings, but did not see any new gardens. He thought, "I will look tomorrow."

The next morning, Raven saw smaller buildings with grass in front of them. He saw people too. He flew up into a tree's branches looking for seeds.

Raven saw some flowers in front of a building. And he found seeds! He ate and ate until he was full, and there were still seeds left.

He thought, "I think I can stay here and eat seeds for many days." He went to sleep in a tree and slept all night.

The next morning Raven found no seeds. He saw four squirrels running. One squirrel had a full mouth. Raven knew where the seeds had gone.

Raven followed the squirrel. The squirrel ran
into a hole in the tree where Raven had slept.
Now Raven knew where he could find some
more seeds.

After the squirrel was gone, Raven found many seeds in the hole. He ate and then flew back up into the tree to take a nap.

Raven was awakened by loud chattering.
He saw a squirrel climb to the branch where
he was. The squirrel sounded like it was saying,
"Thief! Thief!"

Raven knew he had to go looking for a new place to find food. He found a market with boxes of cherries sitting out front. Cherries were his favorite fruit!

Raven ate two cherries. As he reached
for another one, the woman who owned
the market chased him away. He went back
and took just enough cherries for the day.

The woman came out again and said,
"Thief! Thief!" and put a wire cover over the
boxes. The next morning Raven went back,
lifted the wire and stole more cherries.

Raven saw a boy and a girl fill a bag with cherries. They went inside the market to pay for them. Raven took some cherries before the children came back.

When the children walked home, Raven flew along. They sat on the front steps of their house and ate cherries. Raven sat down on the sidewalk. They watched each other eat cherries.

When he finished his cherries, Raven stood in front of the children. He cocked his head to the right and left. He hopped around. The children gave Raven cherries.

The children ran around to the back of the
house. Raven followed them and saw a garden
full of flowers and vegetables. Raven decided
to stay there for the night.

In the morning the children brought him a bowl of cherries. He was glad he had explored the city, but Raven missed his quiet home in the orchard. It was time to go home!

WORDS TO KNOW

cherries

squirrel

sunflowers

INDEX